ST. PATRICK'S DAY
FROM THE
BLACK LAGOON®

Get more monster-sized laughs from

The Black Lagoon®

#1: The Class Trip from the Black Lagoon

#2: The Talent Show from the Black Lagoon

#3: The Class Election from the Black Lagoon

#4: The Science Fair from the Black Lagoon

#5: The Halloween Party from the Black Lagoon

#6: The Field Day from the Black Lagoon

#7: The School Carnival from the Black Lagoon

#8: Valentine's Day from the Black Lagoon

#9: The Christmas Party from the Black Lagoon

#10: The Little League Team from the Black Lagoon

#11: The Snow Day from the Black Lagoon

#12: April Fools' Day from the Black Lagoon

#13: Back-to-School Fright from the Black Lagoon

#14: The New Year's Eve Sleepover from the Black Lagoon

#15: The Spring Dance from the Black Lagoon

#16: The Thanksgiving Day from the Black Lagoon

#17: The Summer Vacation from the Black Lagoon

#18: The Author Visit from the Black Lagoon

SUN ⟶

ST. PATRICK'S DAY
FROM THE
BLACK LAGOON®

TOP OF THE MORNING TO YOU, SIR.

THE BLARNEY STONE

GRRR...

by Mike Thaler
Illustrated by Jared Lee

SCHOLASTIC INC.

New York Toronto London Auckland
Sydney Mexico City New Delhi Hong Kong

CIRCLE WITH LEGS

For my Patty, every day.
—M.T.

To Lori Brumley.
—J.L.

ISBN 978-0-545-27328-2

12 11 10 9 8 7 6 5 4 3 2 1   11 12 13 14 15 16/0

Printed in the U.S.A.   40
First printing, February 2011

SIX-LEGGED DOG

CONTENTS

Chapter 1: Coming Attractions 6

Chapter 2: March On 10

Chapter 3: Pinch an Inch 18

Chapter 4: Patty's Day 22

Chapter 5: A Green Dream 26

Chapter 6: Capping the Problem 30

Chapter 7: A Little Shoe Biz 34

Chapter 8: Somewhere Over the Rainbow 40

Chapter 9: A Green Space 46

Chapter 10: Launch Time 52

Chapter 11: Love a Parade 56

WALKS LIKE A TYRANNOSAURUS REX

TWO-LEGGED DOG

CHAPTER 1
COMING ATTRACTIONS

Today Mrs. Green announced that St. Patrick's Day is a week away. I don't know much about that holiday except that we don't

GREEN TEA

← WARTHOG (VERY MEAN)

get off from school and we are all supposed to wear something green. Mrs. Green is already set for sure.

ST. PATRICK →

What do I have that's green? I have old underwear. I guess that won't work. I don't have much else. I'm really in a pickle. That's it. I could be a pickle! Well, at least I've got a whole week to think about it.

RUBBER PICKLE SUIT →

← HUBIE

(A) PINK AND RED

(B) BLUE AND YELLOW

(C) BLACK AND BLUE

(D) PURPLE AND BROWN

ANSWER ON PAGE 10

CHAPTER 2
MARCH ON

LEPRECHAUN MARCHING

We're going to have a parade. Mrs. Green says we can dress up as lots of things, perhaps a leprechaun.

I LOVE A PARADE.

KID FROM ANOTHER CLASS

10

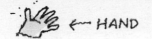
← HAND

Eric raises his hand. "Is that a kind of leopard?"

"No," answers Mrs. Green. "More like an elf," she continues.

A LEOPARD IS VERY FAST.

I THOUGHT AN ELF WAS TALLER AND HELPED SANTA CLAUS BUILD THE TOYS AND TAKE CARE OF THE REINDEER.

DITTO.

11

Eric raises his hand again.

"But I can't sing," he says.

"Elves don't sing," states Mrs. Green.

"Elves Presley does," declares Eric with a big smile.

After we're done laughing and Eric has left for the principal's office, Mrs. Green continues.

14

"You can also be a four-leaf clover, a rainbow, a pot of gold, or a shamrock."

15

I think of asking if I can be a sham–rock and roll, but decide that silence is the best principle.

CHAPTER 3
PINCH AN INCH

TONE IT DOWN, KIDS. I HAVE A SMASHING HEADACHE.

On the school bus home, everyone's talking about what green thing they're going to wear. Doris has a dance dress, Freddy has a chef's hat, Derek has a football jersey, and Penny has a velvet ribbon. They are all set and I am green with envy.

← WEIRD KID FROM ANOTHER SCHOOL

GREEN PIZZA

DORIS

FREDDY

DEREK

PENNY

19

YOU'RE EMBARRASSING.

Eric says if you're not wearing something green, everyone can pinch you. Then he smiles and makes pinching motions with both hands in the air. I wonder what I can wear so that I'll be pinch-proof.

ERIC, SIT DOWN.

ERIC IS SO ANNOYING.

20

OTHER OBJECTS YOU CAN FIND AT THE END OF A RAINBOW

LOST BASEBALLS

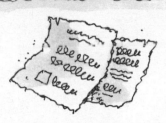

YOUR HOMEWORK

POT OF COFFEE

OLD ITCHY CHRISTMAS SWEATER

COMIC BOOKS

MOM'S CELL PHONE

CHAPTER 4

PATTY'S DAY

When I get home, I tell Mom my dilemma. We put on our thinking caps. Unfortunately, they're not green. Mom knows all about St. Patrick's Day. It started a long time ago in Ireland. St. Patrick drove all the snakes out of Ireland. He must have had a big car.

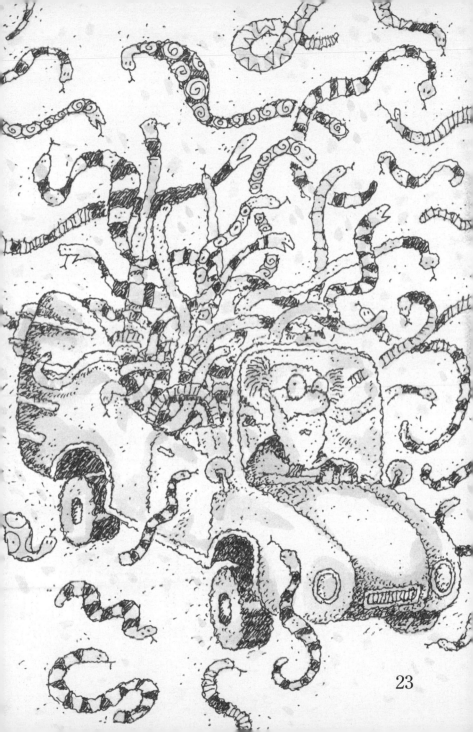

He also brought the first book to Ireland. He was sort of an early librarian. I bet Mrs. Beamster knew him. The most important thing is the kids in Ireland do get the day off from school. Life is not fair. And, I still have a mean green problem.

HUBIE, ST. PATRICK WAS A LITTLE BEFORE MY TIME.

OH...

GEE...

25

CHAPTER 5
A GREEN DREAM

Before I go to bed, I look through my drawers and my closet. Mom says it's a good opportunity to straighten up. Bummer. I like this holiday less and less, so I just go to bed. Bad move because I have a greenmare.

It's St. Patrick's Day and everything in the world is green. The sky, the sun, the houses, the cars, and all the people. I'm the only thing that's not.

Everyone is chasing me, making pinching motions in the air. Even the snakes are chasing me. I wake up and pinch myself to see if I'm still dreaming.

29

CHAPTER 6
CAPPING
THE PROBLEM

The next day on the school bus, I look out the window and see a big billboard that says GO GREEN.

← RUNNER

THINGS HUBIE CAN DO TO "GO GREEN"

DON'T BREATHE AS MUCH

RECYCLE HOMEWORK

BATHE DOG LESS

WALK TO SCHOOL

TURN OFF LIGHTS

31

This is too much. In art class, I ask Miss Swamp for green construction paper. She brings some over and shows me how to make a leprechaun cap. It looks a little weird, but it will do in a pinch. Now I'm ready to face St. Patrick's Day.

CHAPTER 7

A LITTLE SHOE BIZ

Mrs. Beamster didn't know St. Patrick, but she knows all about leprechauns. They are little old men about two feet tall, who dress all in green, wear leather aprons and little caps like mine, and make tiny shoes. They earn pots of gold — I guess there are lots of people with small feet.

GOLD → 🌞 SILVER → 🌑

← COMPUTER VIRUS

← BOOKWORM

35

Instead of putting it in a bank, they hide the gold at the end of a rainbow. I guess they can't reach the teller window. They don't get much interest, but it's a colorful investment.

RAINBOW

BEGINNING

END

THERE IT IS.

FINALLY.

THESE BAGS ARE GETTING HEAVY.

37

Mrs. Beamster says the way to find a leprechaun is to follow the sound of his little hammer tapping on shoes. Eric starts hitting his pencil on the bottom of the table, and everyone spends the rest of the period looking for a leprechaun.

BUG →

HALF A BUG →

38

39

CHAPTER 8
SOMEWHERE OVER THE RAINBOW

SHOWERS

TWO BUGS →

At the end of the day, there's a spring shower. When we get out of school, there's a rainbow. I decide to find the end of it and see if there's really a pot of gold there. Eric, Derek, Randy, and Doris all say they're going to walk home. We wave good-bye and go our separate ways.

40

TINY DOG →

← BARKING

41

I duck between houses, climb over fences, and go down alleys. Every so often I see one of my friends doing the same thing. At the end of the day, we all run into each other. We all have muddy shoes and are dead tired. We all agree rainbows may have an end or two, but none of us could find them.

START

HUBIE'S ROUTE

CONTINUED →

43

We all go together to the ice cream store, pool our leftover lunch money, and get a waffle cone with two scoops of rainbow ice cream. We all get our licks in and are as happy as if we found the pot of gold. Instead, we have a potluck, or a pot-lick.

ST. PATRICK'S DAY POTLUCK DISHES

CORNED BEEF AND CABBAGE

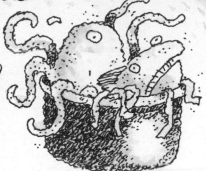

FISHY IRISH STEW

COLCANNON

FORFAR BRIDIES

ANGELS ON HORSEBACK

BLACK PUDDING OR BLOOD SAUSAGE

CHAPTER 9

A GREEN SPACE

The big day is finally here. I put on my leprechaun cap and wait for the school bus. When it pulls up, T-Rex is wearing green suspenders. On the way to school, I'm glad he doesn't pretend all the stoplights are green.

CURB

When we get to school, Mr. Bender, the principal, is wearing a green tie and Mrs. Green's room is decorated with rainbow streamers and yellow and green

balloons. There are little green footprints all over the school, and we follow them looking for four-leaf clovers and little rocks painted gold.

Mrs. Green says we can use the rocks to buy treats in the cafeteria and that four-leaf clovers will bring good luck.

OTHER THINGS THAT BRING GOOD LUCK

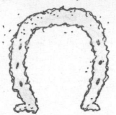

HORSESHOE

RABBIT'S FOOT

ACORN

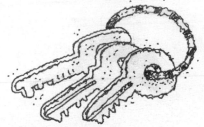

THREE KEYS

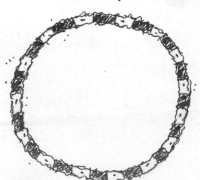

LUCKY CHARM BRACELET

SHINY PENNY

GREEN HAMBURGER →

CHAPTER 10
LAUNCH TIME

The cafeteria is something else. Miss Belch has hung green shamrocks all around and put out green tablecloths, green plates, and green napkins.

GREEN PIZZA →

And the food! We have green hamburgers, green pizza, green mashed potatoes, green pudding, green cookies, and green milk.

FRESH GREEN PUKE

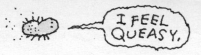

I pass on the green milk, but Freddy eats everything, plus seconds. Then he turns green and runs to the bathroom.

GREEN THINGS NOT TO EAT

FROGS

POISON IVY

BROCCOLI

CATERPILLAR

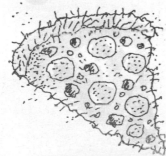

MOLDY PIZZA

BOOGERS

GREEN   RED

CHAPTER 11

LOVE A PARADE

After lunch, we all get into our costumes.

Eric is a leopard, Doris is a fairy godmother, Penny is a harp, and me, Derek, and Freddy are a rainbow. Freddy is the green part.

FACT: THERE IS EVIDENCE OF PARADES IN CAVE PAINTINGS 3,000 YEARS OLD.

We march up and down the hall singing "When Irish Eyes Are Smiling" and go into all the classrooms handing out candy kisses. It is a great day. I even found a four-leaf clover. Someday, I'm sure I'll find the end of the rainbow.

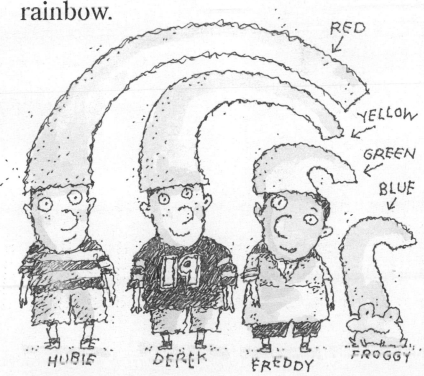

RED
YELLOW
GREEN
BLUE

HUBIE   DEREK   FREDDY   FROGGY

AFTER KISSING THE BLARNEY STONE
I'VE TURNED INTO A MOTORMOUTH!
TALK TALK TALK
HA HA HA
I CAN'T STOP BLABBING!
BLAB BLAB BLAB
HA HA HA
HA HA HA
HA HA HA
I'M A LAUGHING HYENA!
HA HA HA
HA HA HA
THATS FUNNY!
HA HA
BLARNEY STONE
HYENA: WOLFLIKE ANIMAL FROM AFRICA AND ASIA.

LEPRECHAUN JOKES

WHEN DO LEPRECHAUNS CROSS THE STREET?

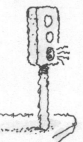

LET'S GO.

WHEN THE LIGHT'S GREEN

HOW DO YOU KNOW WHEN A LEPRECHAUN IS JEALOUS?

I LOVE YOUR NEW HAT.

THANKS. WHY IS YOUR FACE GREEN?

WHEN HE'S GREEN WITH ENVY

WHAT DO YOU CALL A LEPRECHAUN WHO CHANGES YOUR OIL?

A LUBRICHAUN

WHAT KIND OF COMPUTER DOES A LEPRECHAUN USE?

A LEP-TOP

HOW DO LEPRECHAUNS TIE UP PACKAGES?

WITH RAINBOWS

ST. PATRICK'S DAY RIDDLE

"Knock knock."

"Who's there?"

"Irish."

"Irish who?"

"Irish you a happy St. Patrick's Day!"